This book belongs to:

_____

Jim Carrey

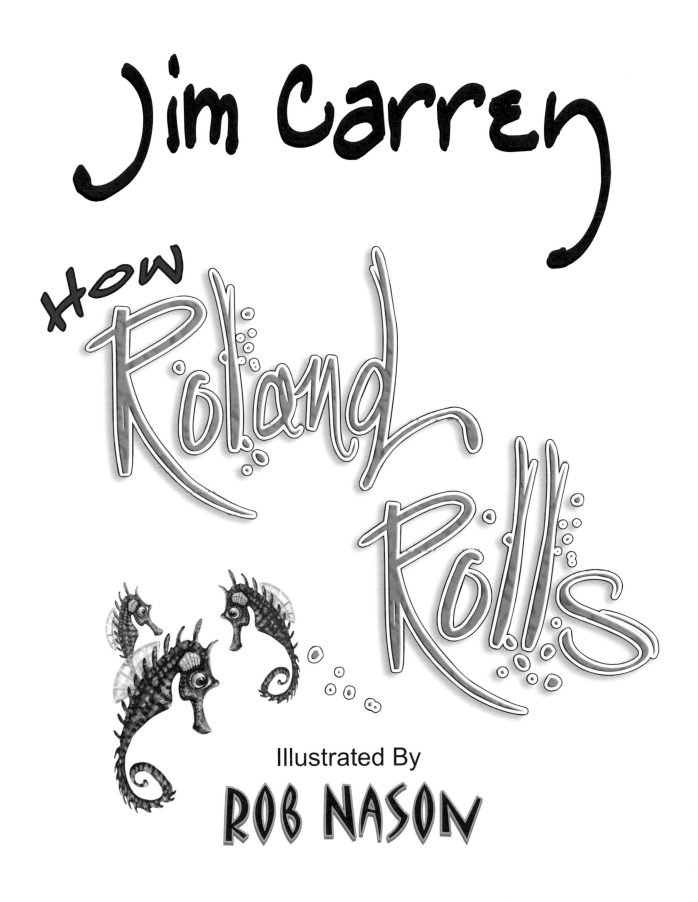

How Roland Rolls

Illustrated By

ROB NASON

For Jackson

How Roland Rolls
By Jim Carrey
Illustrated by Rob Nason

Copyright © 2013 by Some Kind of Garden, Inc., Los Angeles, California

Published in the United States by:
Some Kind of Garden Media
Los Angeles, CA

Distributed in the United States and Canada by Perseus Distribution www.perseusdistribution.com.

Book Shepherd / Project Manager: John Raatz, The Visioneering Group, www.thevisioneeringgroup.com
Illustrations, Book and Jacket Design: R. C. Nason

Some Kind of Garden Media books may be purchased for educational, business, or sales promotional use. For information, please write: info@skogarden.com.

Library of Congress Cataloguing-in-Publication Data
Carrey, Jim.
How Roland rolls / Jim Carrey.
ISBN 978-0-9893680-0-1 (hardcover)
1. JUVENILE FICTION / Visionary & Metaphysical

Library of Congress Control Number: 2013940248

First printing, June, 2013

Printed in Canada

Jim Carrey

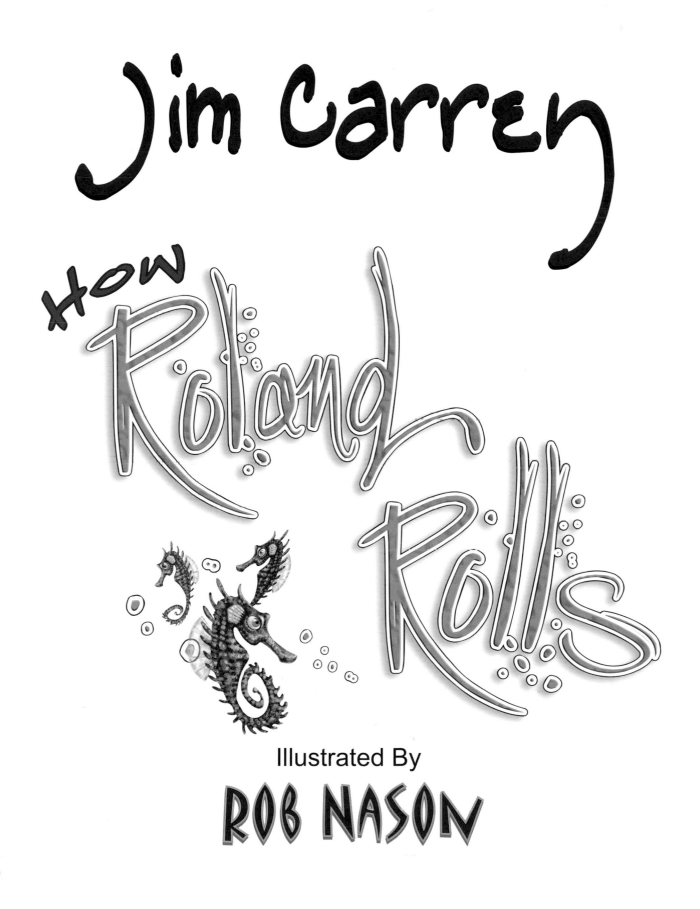

How Roland Rolls

Illustrated By
ROB NASON

Some Kind of Garden Media

Somewhere...

in the middle of the
deep blue sea,

a wave named Roland
came to be.

But one day a
big ship cut right
in between them

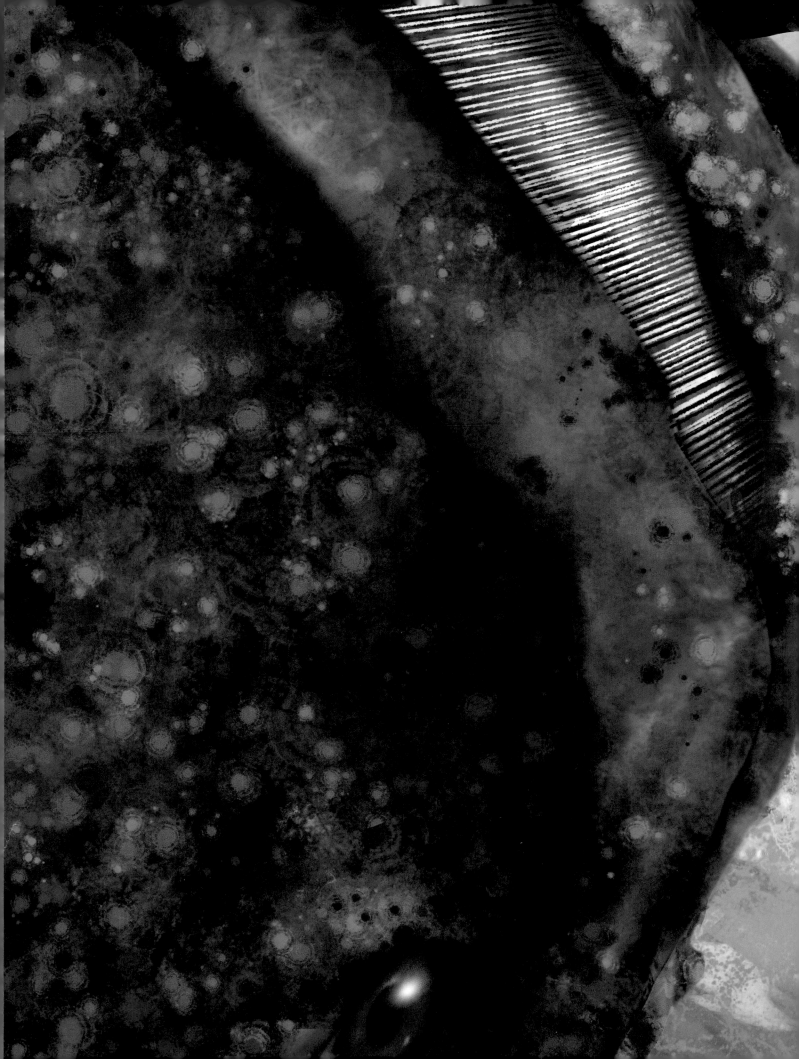

That's when a whale jumped way
up in the air,

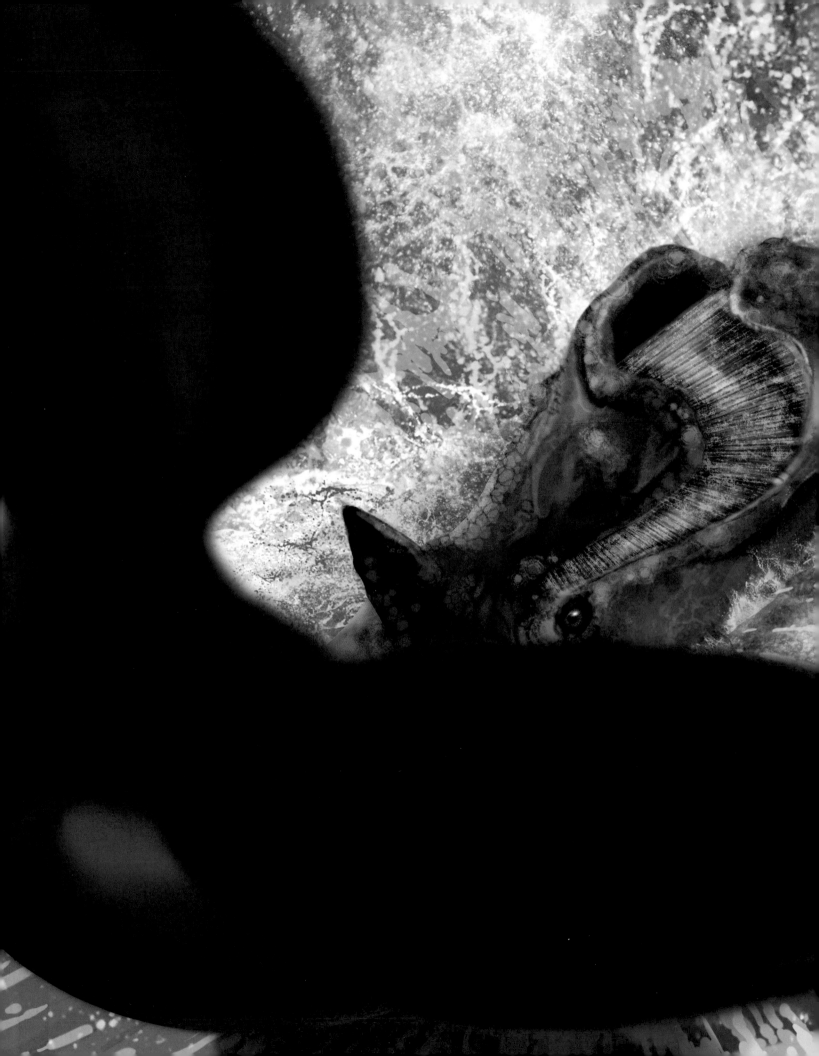

and when he came
down Roland was

splashed
everywhere!

Poor Roland felt lonely.

He cried salty tears,
and soon he was facing the
worst of his *fears...*

A wave they called Gnarly, using maximum

Suction,

could suck Roland up and cause major Destruction!

But after chewing on a sailboat,
old Gnarly calmed down

And the sailboat
was lost, but the
sailors were found.

With a wave of relief,
soon Roland was met

by a funny old sea bird
who loved to get wet.

His old feathers tickled,
their new friendship grew.

And the old bird introduced
him to a wave that he knew.

Her name was *Shimmer*
because up on her crest,
the sun made her glimmer
like he liked her the best.

And they rolled on together for thousands of days.

They made thousands of ripples that went thousands of ways.

Yes, Roland and Shimmer
thought love was just grand,

but then Roland was told
that life ends in the sand,

That the coast is a place
that a wave can't go past,

unless you're like GNARLY

and even then you won't last!

So the day they saw land
it gave them both such a fright,

**But Roland kept rollin'
and Shimmer stayed**

And they crashed on the beach

together that Night.

Now, they thought
it would hurt
when they got
mixed together,

yet it just seemed to tickle
like the old sea bird's feather.

They didn't feel different
just bigger somehow,
like the fish were all swimming
inside of them now.

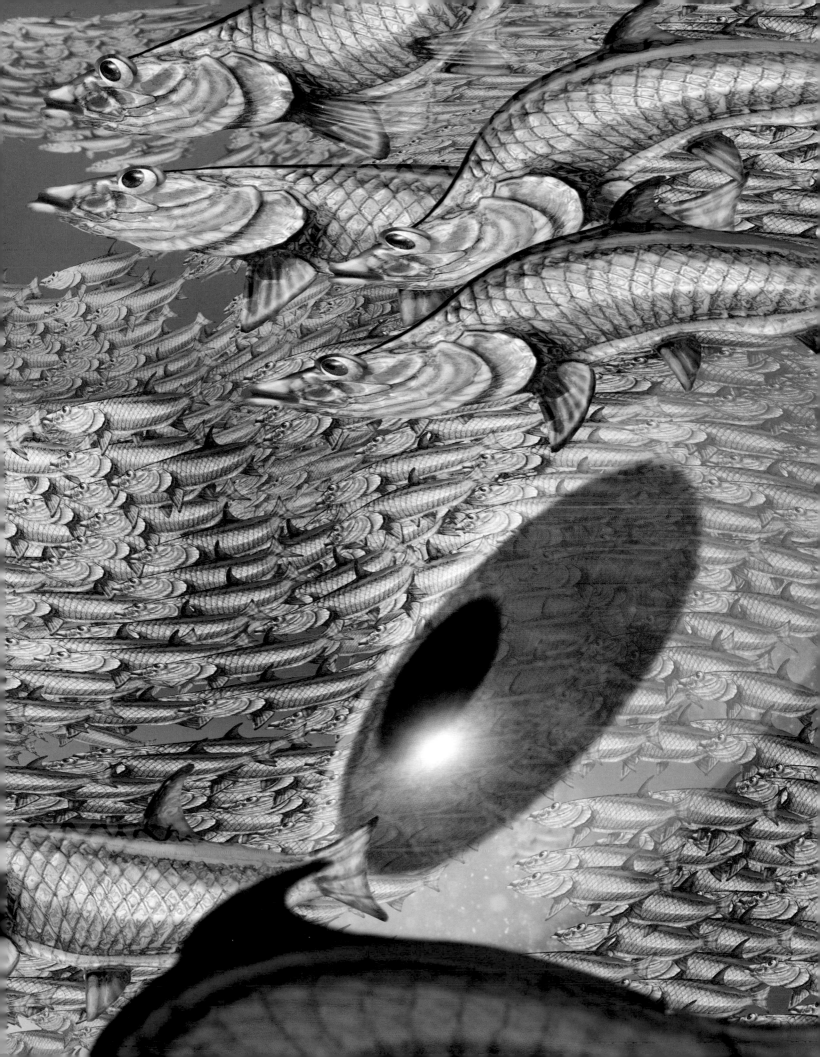

Then down they went... Woosh
in one *SWOOSHY* motion!

And when they got deep
they were struck by a notion --

"We're not little waves,
we're this whole

BIG

WIDE

Ocean!"

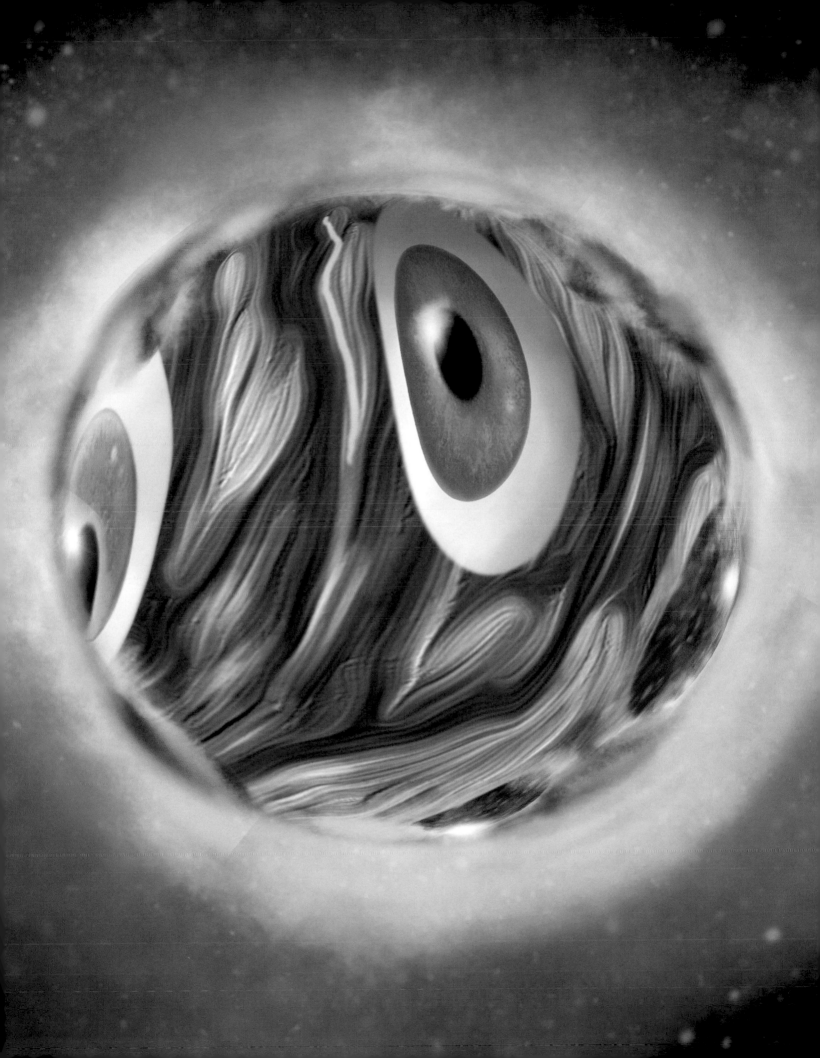

**And suddenly
every wave they ever knew
was right there to greet them,**

and the ripples came, too.

And they saw that together they played a much bigger role --

they were in every ice cube between the North and South Pole...

In all of the rivers,

and all of the streams...

The puddles,

the pools,

and mom's iron
when it steams.

They fill up
the sink
that you
wash your
bowl in,

and when you're sad,
even your tears are
Roland.

NOW, ROLAND HAS EVERYTHING,

WHICH WAS ONE OF HIS GOALS,

Like Roland and Shimmer
you will always belong,

if you think you're just
one little wave...
you're just wrong.

You're like Roland,

and you'll *always* be rollin' along.

THE EN

Jim made these faces so that Rob could draw Roland!

Can you make *Roland's* face?

Take a picture of <u>your</u> Roland face and upload it to:
www.howrolandrolls.com

Acknowledgments

It may not take a village to produce a children's book, but you sure can't do it alone. I want to extend my deepest thanks to everyone who helped make How Roland Rolls happen, but especially to –

Dr. Seuss – who very early on became a part of my DNA. I have to blame someone!

Jane and Jackson – my glorious daughter and grandson – who are for me, the answer to one of life's most important questions - "Why am I here?"

John Raatz – for his unending perseverance and his willingness to boldly take Starship Carrey to a place where it has never gone before.

Rob Nason – whose vibrant and electric images brought the characters to life and completely surpassed expectation.

Thanks to Linda, Nicole, Michael, Whitney and the rest of my staff at Some Kind of Garden for the years of support, day in, day out.

My father, Percy, who could tell a bedtime story like no one else on earth, and all my family in Canada. I hope the kids enjoy Roland!

My mum, Kathleen, Jane's mom, Melissa, Jenny and moms everywhere, whose gentle hugs are the last thing standing between us and oblivion.

My friend, Jeff Foster, for his kindness, insight and encouragement.

Evan Asher – who will always be in my heart.

John Rigney, Jimmy Miller, Eric Gold, Dan Aloni, Ari Emanuel, Marleah Leslie, Debbie Klein and the rest of my wonderful team.

David Langer, Benjamin Cziller and Zach Brewer Ball, for their creative contributions

Elise Gochberg, Doug Symington, Danny Klassen and everyone at Friesens Canada. Sabrina McCarthy, Jessica Schmidt and the team at Perseus Distribution US. Roland was printed in Canada and distributed in the US – just like me!

All of the visionary teachers who fly above the waves so the rest of us can see more clearly.

And lastly, I want to thank faith and fate for being so kind to me.

– Jim Carrey

Acknowledgments

To my wife, Nancy, the sweetest girl to crash my shores.

Mum & Dad – for pointing me in the right direction and nurturing my sense of adventure.

Family and friends – who never stop believing in me; should know… you inspire me.

The children in my life, Nick, Code, Ciara, Hanna, Tim, Amanda, Winni, Mason, Maddie, Cooper, Charlie, Mia, Maya, Jinsey, Emery, Michael, Coupe and Tatum for refreshing the seven year-old in me.

Jim Carrey – for your engaging creative process... the catalyst into an enchanting world of wonderment. A genius and stand-alone Director I am honored to work with.

John Raatz – for finding me and keeping the stars aligned.

– Rob Nason